Art A to Z

Smithsonian Institution

With love to my sister-in-law Lynn, whose artistic talent doesn't go unnoticed.—LGG

This book is dedicated to my mother, Nancy Tabbutt—ST

Lyrics and performance by Tish Rabe
Musical Arrangement by Bruce Zimmerman
Produced by Edge Studio

Published by Soundprints, an imprint of Palm Publishing, LLC, Norwalk, Connecticut.
www.soundprints.com

Written by Laura Gates Galvin
Illustrations by Steven Tabbutt

Editor: Barbie Heit
Book design: Meredith Campbell Britton
Production: Chris Dobias

First Edition 2012
10 9 8 7 6 5 4 3 2 1
Manufactured in China

Acknowledgments:
    Our very special thanks to Diane Kidd, Education Specialist, for her curatorial review of this title.
    Soundprints would also like to thank Ellen Nanney and Kealy Wilson at the Smithsonian Institution's Office of
Product Development and Licensing for their help in the creation of this book.

Library of Congress Cataloging-in-Publication Data

Galvin, Laura Gates, 1963-
Art A to Z / by Laura Gates Galvin ; illustrated by Steven Tabbutt. -- 1st ed.
    p. cm.
ISBN 978-1-60727-196-3 (pbk.)
1. Art—Juvenile literature. 2. Alphabet books.
I. Tabbutt, Steven. II. Title.
 N7440.G35 2011
 700—dc22
                                        2011016603

To **download** your
audiobook and activities
included with your
purchase of this book:

1) Go to **www.soundprints.com**

2) Click on the "CLAIM MY DOWNLOAD"
button at the top left of the home page

3) Follow the directions to download
your free audiobook and activities!

Art A to Z

by Laura Gates Galvin

Illustrated by Steven Tabbutt

Soundprints

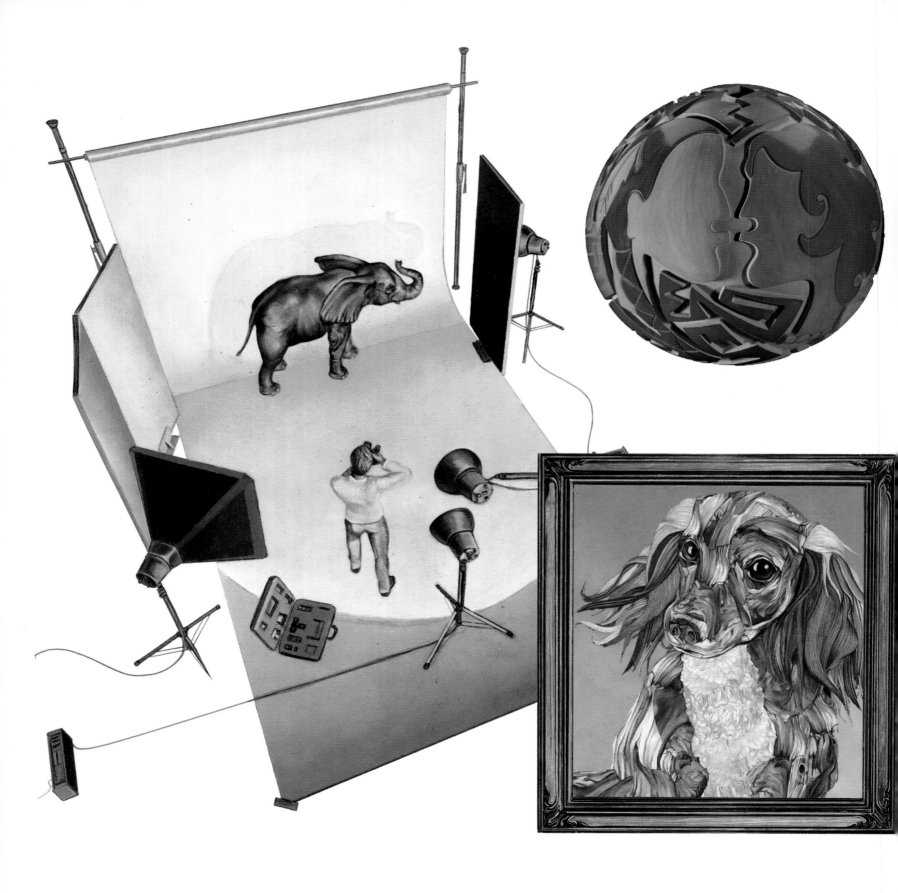

A is for **Art**

Art can be created
in many different ways—
through paintings, sculptures, photographs
and pottery with glaze.

Bb

B is for **Brushstroke**

A line made by a paintbrush,
whether narrow or quite wide,
is called a painter's brushstroke,
and with it paint's applied.

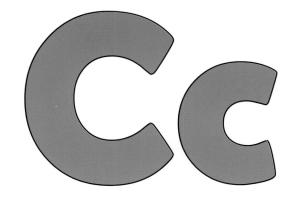

C is for **Collage**

Cut out pictures, fabric or paper,
arrange them so they look just great.
Paste them down and you'll be proud
of the collage that you create.

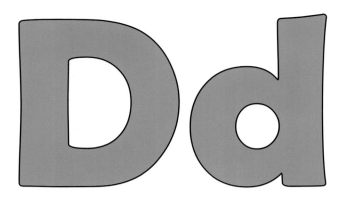

D is for Digital Art

Making pictures on a computer
is called digital art.
If you have the right software,
you'll be ready to start!

E is for Egyptian Art

Egyptian art dates back
many thousands of years ago.
Pottery, statues and pyramids
are some types that we know.

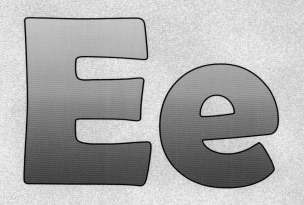

F is for Finger Painting

There are different ways to paint—
finger painting is just one.
Use your fingers like a paintbrush,
you're sure to have some fun!

G is for Greek Art

Statues of gods and goddesses
were created in ancient Greece.
Some of them are so old
that they're no longer in one piece.

H is for Hokusai

An influential artist
and a very famous man,
Hokusai painted people,
scenes and legends of Japan.

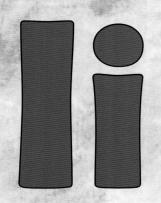

I is for Impressionism

Monet, Degas and Pissarro
painted scenes of day and night.
These impressionistic artists
made use of color and light.

J is for Jewelry

Jewelry-making is creating
rings, necklaces and more!
Jewelry is often seen at craft fairs,
or sold in a special store.

K is for Kinetic Art

A three-dimensional creation that has motion or a moving part, like a sculpture or a mobile, is called kinetic art.

L is for Landscape

Mountains, fields and valleys,
make a pretty landscape view!
The trees are different shades of green
and the sky can be bright blue.

Mm

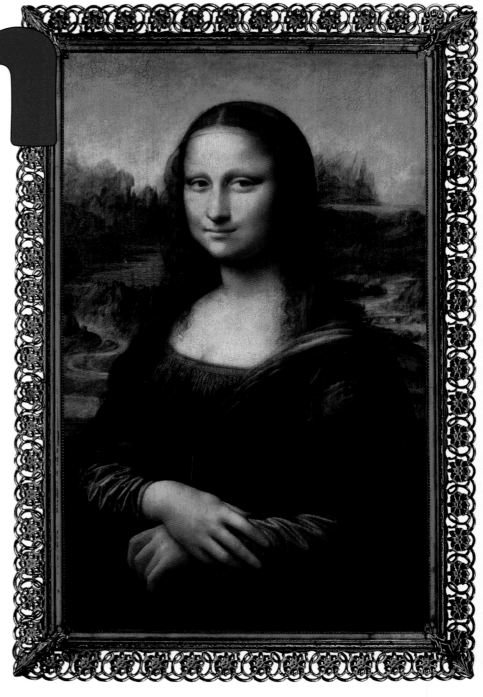

M is for Mona Lisa

The *Mona Lisa* is a portrait
of a woman with a smile.
It was painted by DaVinci.
Renaissance was his style.

N is for **Native American Art**

Types of Native American art are pots made out of clay, moccasins, palmetto dolls, and instruments to play.

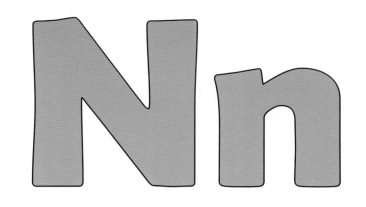

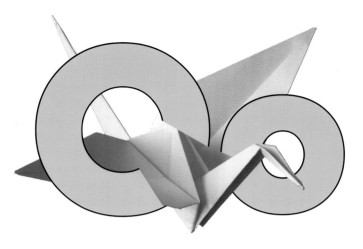

O is for Origami

The art of origami
started in Japan.
Paper is folded into an object,
like a bird, fish or fan.

P is for Primary Colors

The primary colors
are yellow, red and blue.
You'll get a secondary color
if you try mixing two.

P p

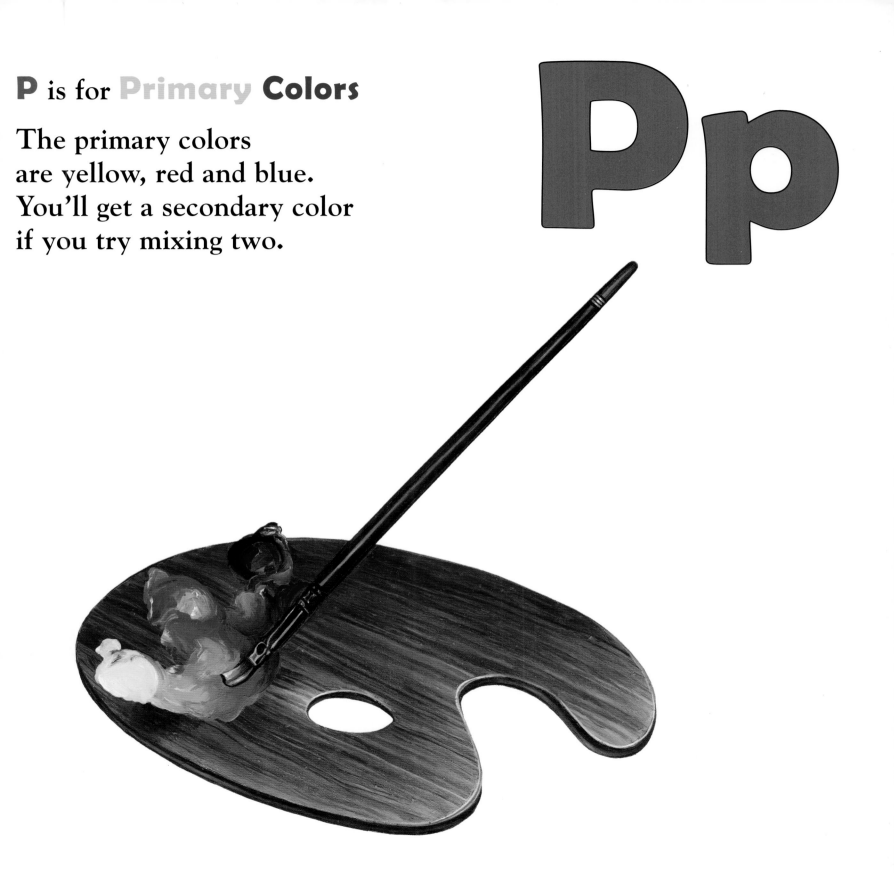

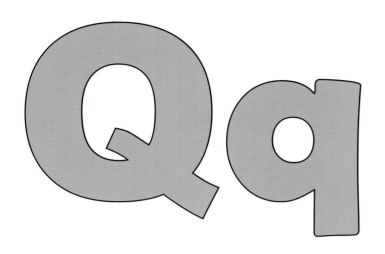

Q is for Quilting

Quilts are sewn to cover beds,
or hung up for all to see.
In early American times,
women made them at a quilting bee.

R is for **Realism**

Artists of the realistic school
choose subjects they see every day,
then they paint the people or objects
in a very accurate way.

S is for Sculpture

A sculpture is a figure
that you chisel, carve or mold.
It can be made of such material
as bronze, wood, clay or gold.

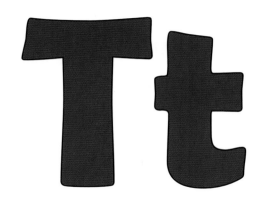

T is for **The Thinker**

This statue is called *The Thinker*. It's a man with a serious face. It was the first piece by Rodin to be shown in a public place.

U is for Upholstery

Sometimes fabric and padding
cover furniture, like a chair.
When applied, it's called upholstery,
and it's done with skill and care.

V is for van Gogh

Sunflowers and *The Starry Night* may be paintings that you know. They were created by a famous artist, the great Vincent van Gogh.

W is for Watercolor

Watercolor is a type of paint.
It has a transparent look.
Watercolor art can be found
in a museum, gallery or book.

X is for **Xylography**

This ancient form of printmaking
was very complicated.
Artists carved a stamp from wood
and images were created.

Yy

Y is for Yarn

Artwork using colored yarn dates back to long ago, made by a group of people native to Mexico.

Wapaas (root basket), Vivian "Stu yat" Harrison (Yakama), Toppenish, Washington, 2003, National Museum of the American Indian, Smithsonian Institution

Z is for **Zoom Lens**

A photographer is an artist
who doesn't use paint or pens.
She can focus on faraway objects
with her camera that has a zoom lens.

Glossary

ART Art is a form of creative expression that can be applied in different ways, such as painting, drawing and sculpting. Some art is displayed in galleries and museums for people to see and admire, but you don't have to be a professional artist to create your own masterpiece.

BRUSHSTROKE When a paintbrush is dipped in paint and then a line is made with the paintbrush on canvas or paper, it is called a brushstroke. The lines can be wide or narrow, short or long.

COLLAGE A collage is a piece of art that is made by arranging cut-out images from magazines, photographs, or pieces of paper or fabric in a decorative way. The pieces are then glued down to a hard surface, such as wood, paper, cardboard or canvas. Some collages contain three-dimensional objects, too.

DIGITAL ART One of the newest forms of art is called digital art and it is created on a computer. Software allows a person to make a picture, or change existing pictures, using tools on the computer instead of more traditional physical tools like pens, pencils and paintbrushes.

EGYPTIAN ART Egyptian art was created long ago and it refers to everything from hieroglyphics on temples to the great pyramids, to pottery and statues. Much Egyptian art tells a story about someone's life and their journey into the afterlife.

FINGER PAINTING The only thing needed for finger painting is paper, paint, and of course, fingers. Most people, at some point in their lives, have probably tried finger painting.

GREEK ART Greek art includes vases, statues, jewelry, painting, pottery and architecture. This art was created thousands of years ago. Amazingly, many pieces have survived through all of this time.

HOKUSAI Katsushika Hokusai was a Japanese painter and printmaker. He is most famous for his series of prints called *Thirty-Six Views of Mount Fuji*. One of these views, *The Great Wave off Kangawa*, has become very well-known, both in Japan and throughout the world.

IMPRESSIONISM Impressionism began in France in the 1860s and it was a new way for artists to interpret subject matter. Impressionism allowed artists to use the effects of color and light to capture the overall impressions of scenes and subjects.

JEWELRY Jewelry-making is a form of art that has been around for a very long time. The first known jewelry was made of natural materials that were easily found, like stones, shells, wood and even bones from animals. Today, jewelry is still made from natural materials but also from man-made materials such as plastic, nylon or found objects.

KINETIC ART Kinetic art is a three-dimensional art style in which there are moving parts. One of the pioneers of kinetic art is a man named Alexander Calder, who in the 1930s started making abstract sculptures known as mobiles and stabiles. Some of his pieces were powered by motors, but others were so light they were set in motion by the slightest breeze.

LANDSCAPE Landscape is a very popular subject of art. Artists are inspired by their surroundings and often take their canvases and paints outside to paint exactly what they are seeing.

MONA LISA The *Mona Lisa* is one of the most popular paintings in the world and it is quite small. It is believed that Leonardo da Vinci most likely started painting it in 1503 and finished it about four years later. The painting was named after a wealthy businessman's wife whose name was Lisa Gherardini. Mona means "my lady" or "madam," so Mona Lisa means Madam Lisa. The portrait is displayed in the Louvre Museum in Paris, France.

NATIVE AMERICAN ART Native American art is rich in culture and symbolism and is included in every part of Native American life. Examples of Native American art are woven baskets, clothing, jewelry, masks and musical instruments such as drums and rattles. Each art piece tells a story. Native American art is on display at the National Museum of the American Indian at the Smithsonian Institution in Washington, D.C., and various other museums throughout the United States.

ORIGAMI The centuries-old art of paper-folding is called origami. It originated in Japan and has remained an important part of the Japanese culture. Directions for folding origami have been passed down from generation to generation. Over time, there have been different purposes for origami, such as decorations and tokens of celebrations, peace and good luck.

PRIMARY COLORS There are three primary colors: yellow, blue and red. Primary colors cannot be made from mixing any other colors, but they are the basis for creating all other colors. For example, blue and yellow mixed together make green. Color mixing can be used to create different hues of color, depending on how little or how much of the primary colors are used.

QUILTING Quilting in America began in the 1700s and grew to be popular in the mid-1800s when fabric became more readily available. Later in the century, women gathered for quilting bees where they would help friends finish quilts, socialize and exchange recipes.

REALISM The Realism movement of art began around 1830. Artists painted everyday subjects in a straightforward manner without using their imagination or embellishment to ensure that their paintings looked very realistic.

SCULPTURE Sculptures have been made for thousands of years. In the past, these three-dimensional carvings were made from one or a variety of materials such as clay, wood, marble, bronze, gold or stone. Today, artists use an array of materials that can be soft, hard or man-made to create a sculpture.

THE THINKER French artist Auguste Rodin (1840-1917) created the statue *The Thinker* in 1882. He originally made a small version, called a maquette (ma-ket). In 1904 he made a larger plaster version that was put on display at the Salon in France and two years later in front of the Pantheon, a Roman temple. A bronze version was made in 1925 and can be seen at the Rodin Museum in Philadelphia, Pennsylvania.

UPHOLSTERY When you look at a sofa or chair in your house, you might not think much about the fabric or material covering it. Upholstery uses fabric, threads and the design applied to the fabric by using dyes, embroidery techniques, or printing methods to create art. Upholstering is the act of covering a chair or sofa, which requires a craftsman's skill.

VAN GOGH (1853-1890) Vincent van Gogh was born in Holland in 1853. When he was a young man, he decided to become an artist. He studied art in Belgium and France. He is considered to be an Expressionist artist because he painted from feeling. Sadly, he only sold one painting in his lifetime, *The Red Vineyard*.

WATERCOLOR Watercolor is a pigment or coloring matter that is mixed with water for use as paint. Watercolor can have a transparent look when applied to paper. You simply use a brush and water to apply paint to a particular type of paper made specifically for watercolors. Some famous American watercolorists are Winslow Homer and Andrew Wyeth.

XYLOGRAPHY Xylography was an ancient form of printmaking. Blocks of wood were carved to represent images and then dipped in ink and "stamped" to make an impression. Only the raised part of the engraving would show up when applied so it required a lot of skill to make the carvings on the blocks.

YARN Yarn is a continuous strand of twisted threads of natural or synthetic material, such as wool or nylon, used in weaving or knitting. Traditionally, the yarn is pressed into wax that has been warmed by the sun and is coiled to make patterns, pictures and baskets.

ZOOM LENS A zoom lens is a kind of lens that makes far away objects appear very close, similar to how binoculars and telescopes work. A zoom lens can come in very handy for a photographer when taking photographs of wildlife. The photographer might not be able to get close to the animal but the zoom lens allows a very detailed photograph to be taken so the animal appears to be much closer than it actually is.